NEW PIECES FOR CLARINET: BOOK I

GRADES 3 & 4

GW00467651

A.B.1659

BOLNEY BALLAD

Kenneth V. Jones

EVENING MOOD

Gordon Jacob

SCHERZETTO

Gordon Jacob

EARLY BIRD

Timothy Baxter

A.B. 1659

CAPRICCIO

Raymond Warren

NEW PIECES FOR CLARINET: BOOK I

2

BOLNEY BALLAD

Kenneth V. Jones

EVENING MOOD

Gordon Jacob

SCHERZETTO

Gordon Jacob

EARLY BIRD

Timothy Baxter

CAPRICCIO

BELL PRELUDE

Raymond Warren

PRELUDE

Sebastian Forbes

DANCE IN FIVE

John Lambert

VALSE INGENUE

Gordon Jacob

Printed in England by Caligraving Limited Thetford Norfolk

BELL PRELUDE

Raymond Warren

PRELUDE

Sebastian Forbes

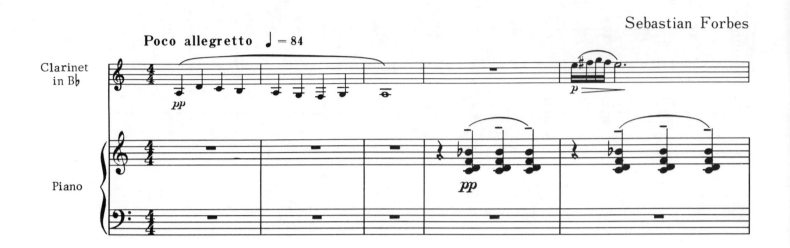

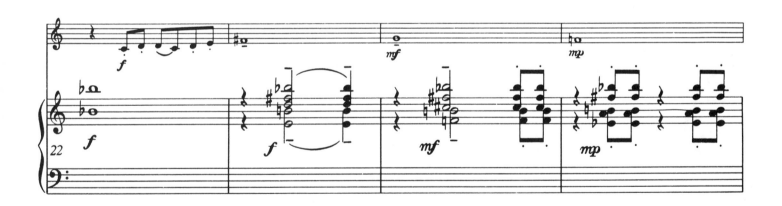

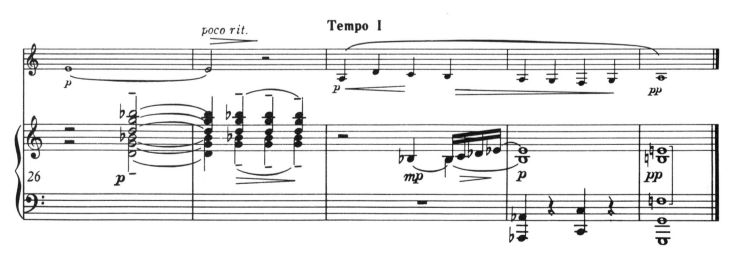

DANCE IN FIVE

John Lambert

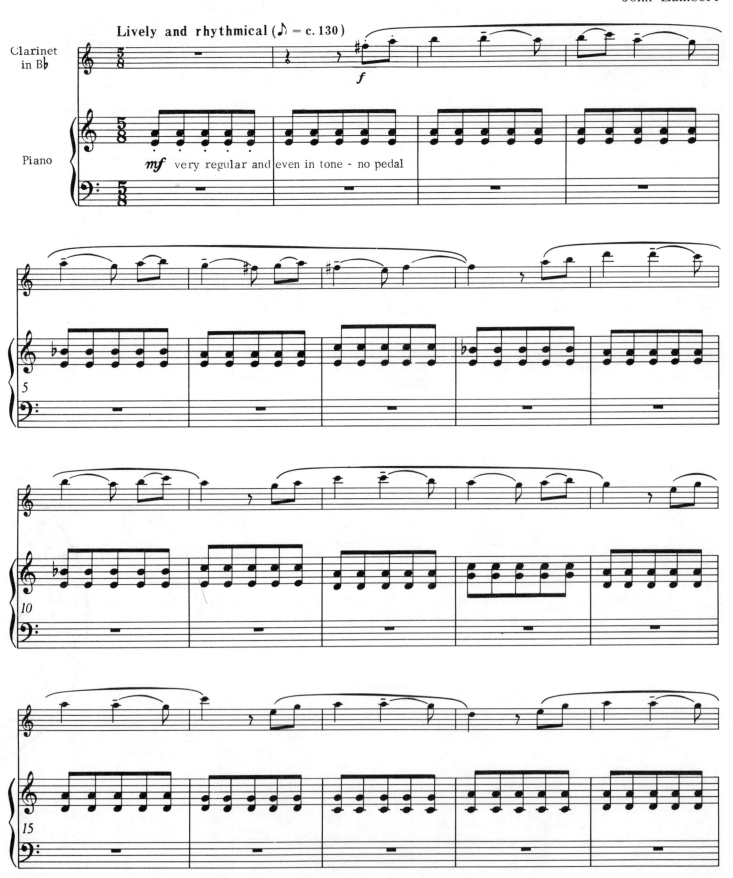

VALSE INGENUE

Gordon Jacob

22

A.B. 1659

Printed in England by Caligraving Limited Thetford Norfolk

The Associated Board's series of new
pieces for wind instruments covers Grades 3—6.
Two books are available for each instrument:
bassoon, clarinet, flute and oboe.

For further details of these pieces
and for a list of all the Board's publications,
please write to the Publishing Department,
14 Bedford Square, London WC1B 3JG.